Frederick J Brown

## A Sketch of the Life of Dr. James McHenry

A paper read before the Maryland Historical Society, November 13th,

1876

Frederick J Brown

**A Sketch of the Life of Dr. James McHenry**
*A paper read before the Maryland Historical Society, November 13th, 1876*

ISBN/EAN: 9783337097400

Printed in Europe, USA, Canada, Australia, Japan

Cover: Foto ©Raphael Reischuk / pixelio.de

More available books at **www.hansebooks.com**

A

# SKETCH OF THE LIFE

OF

# Dr. JAMES McHENRY,

AIDE-DE-CAMP AND PRIVATE SECRETARY OF GENERAL WASHINGTON, AIDE-DE-
CAMP OF MARQUIS DE LA FAYETTE, SECRETARY OF WAR FROM 1796 TO 1800,

A Paper read before the Maryland Historical Society,

November 13th, 1876.

BY

# FREDERICK J. BROWN.

𝕭altimore, 1877.

# A

## SKETCH OF THE LIFE

OF

# Dr. James McHenry.

# Fund-Publication, No. 10.

A

# SKETCH OF THE LIFE

OF

# DR. JAMES MCHENRY,

AIDE-DE-CAMP AND PRIVATE SECRETARY OF GENERAL WASHINGTON, AIDE-DE-CAMP OF MARQUIS DE LA FAYETTE, SECRETARY OF WAR FROM 1796 TO 1800.

A Paper read before the Maryland Historical Society,

November 13th, 1876.

BY

# FREDERICK J. BROWN.

### Baltimore, 1877.

PRINTED BY JOHN MURPHY,
PRINTER TO THE MARYLAND HISTORICAL SOCIETY,
BALTIMORE, 1877.

# A SKETCH OF THE LIFE

OF

# DR. JAMES McHENRY.

JAMES McHENRY, the son of Daniel and Agnes McHenry, was born in Ballymena, county Antrim, Ireland, on the 16th day of November, 1753. Not much is known of his parents. His father was engaged in business in Ballymena, and his affairs were prosperous enough to enable him to send his son James to Dublin to receive a classical education. It is not known how long he had pursued his studies there, when, for the sake of his health, which was not strong, he left them to make a voyage to the American colonies, and came to Baltimore about the year 1771. He was so much struck with the promise which the new country held out, that he wrote to his father urging him to emigrate, and following his advice, his father came out not long afterwards with his younger son John, and established himself in trade on Lovely Lane, in Baltimore. Here his affairs grew with the rapid growth of

2

the town, and the new house was soon engaged
in an importing business of some magnitude.
Meantime the subject of this sketch was, in the
year 1772, at Newark Academy in Delaware, then
a school of much note, following his studies presumably, though it is possible he may have been
not pupil but tutor, and we find him occasionally
indulging in little flights of poetry or at least of
versification, attributable perhaps rather to youth
and rural surroundings than to any decided inspi-
ration. His taste for elegant trifling with the
muses did not, indeed, entirely desert him after
he had arrived at years of discretion, but he made
little claim to the honors of authorship, and kept,
for the most part, for his own amusement or that
of his friends, any accomplishments he may have
had in the way of writing occasional verse.

At what date his academic studies were changed
for professional ones we do not know, but we next
find him studying medicine in Philadelphia under
Dr. Benjamin Rush, who occupied a very high
position in his own profession, and was also to
become eminent both as patriot and as philan-
tropist. It is said in Mr. G. W. Greene's Life
of Nathaniel Greene, that McHenry had studied
medicine rather as a science than as a profession,
which may be true, though we are not aware of
the authority for the statement. McHenry was
still studying with Dr. Rush when the events

which preceded the revolution took place, and, at
a period when two sessions of the General Congress made Philadelphia a remarkable school for
other things besides physic, he was exposed to
all the inspiring influences of the time. Dr. Rush
was on familiar terms with Washington, and there
is good reason to believe that McHenry had here
first the opportunity of forming through personal
acquaintance, that admiration for the hero of the
revolution which he held so strongly all his life.
However that may be, not many weeks after the
Commander-in-Chief set out to take control of the
army at Cambridge, he prepared to follow. Before
going he drew up an informal will in his own
hand, July 29th, 1775. "Being about to set off
for the head-quarters in New England, to serve
as a volunteer, or Surgeon, in the American army,
raised by order of the Continental Congress and
Provincial Conventions, to defend the liberties of
Americans and mankind against the enemies of
both, I therefore resign the disposal of myself and
soul, in all sincerity and lowly reverence, to their
first Giver. And should the events of war number me with the dead, in the name of the dis-
poser of these and all other events, I will and
bequeath," &c. The main provision of the will
was the bequest of "the one-third of the principal
and the one-third of the profit arising from my
partnership with my father Daniel McHenry and

John McHenry, my brother, both of Baltimore Town, Maryland," to be equally divided between his father and brother. He also desired that his "manuscript poetry and other rude sketches" shall all be burnt, and he ended by invoking every form of success for the struggles of liberty, and every possible felicity for "my dear father and brother." The business connection spoken of in the will, between himself and his father and brother, could have been only a nominal one. Instead of his estate being divided between them, as provided in his will, it happened, on the contrary, that he inherited before many years the estates of both, which must have been considerable, as McHenry appears to have lived as a gentleman of leisure after the war and for the rest of his life.

McHenry joined the army as an assistant surgeon, and in January, 1776, was in attendance at the American Hospital at Cambridge. On the 26th day of August, 1776, Congress passed the following resolution: "Resolved that Congress have a proper sense of the merit and services of doctor McHenry, and recommend it to the directors of the different hospitals belonging to the United States, to appoint doctor McHenry to the first vacancy that shall happen of surgeon's berth in any of the said hospitals," and on the next day Dr. Rush sent a copy of the resolution "to Dr. James McHenry, at Mount Washington or New

York," with a letter, to say, "the above resolution of Congress does you as much honor as if they had made you a director of a hospital."[1] On August 10th, 1776, he received from Congress his commission as Surgeon of the Fifth Pennsylvania Battalion, commanded by Colonel Robert Magaw, one of the best disciplined bodies of troops in the army. This battalion, or regiment as it soon afterwards became, was stationed at Fort Washington, and the day after the disastrous battle of Long Island, came down to join the defeated army. On the 29th, Magaw's and Shee's Philadelphia regiments, and the remnants of the Maryland and Delaware commands, which had suffered so severely in the action of the 27th, were all put under General Mifflin, and used to cover the retreat of the American army from Long Island across the river, a most critical service, which was performed with entire success. Soon afterwards Magaw returned to Fort Washington and was put in command, with orders to defend the post to the last extremity. On November 16th, 1776, the fort was attacked by Sir William Howe with a strong force of British and Hessians, and after an obstinate resistance was taken, with more than two thousand prisoners. Among them were McHenry and four

(1) In the possession of J. Howard McHenry, Esq , Baltimore County, of whose collection of original letters, frequent use is made in this sketch.

other surgeons, and their services must have been sorely needed by the wounded prisoners, for the attacking Hessians had marked their victory by wanton atrocity, bayonetting the Americans while they were begging quarter. While thus a prisoner, McHenry addressed a communication to General Howe on the subject of an exchange of prisoners, and in consequence of his application, "Surgeon McHenry" was paroled on January 27th, 1777, and "the sick privates and those who remained of the well were ordered off on parole under my care as Doctor, and the conduct of a British Officer," to Hydestown, New Jersey, whence he reported to General Washington, January 31st. He wrote to the latter asking that he might be freed "as soon as convenient from the restrictions of a parole." The release did not come as soon as he hoped however. He was in Philadelphia, meantime, in the summer of 1777, and was probably in Baltimore during most of the year and until his exchange was effected. On March 5th, 1778, Alexander Hamilton, then aide-de-camp to Washington, wrote to Dr. McHenry from Valley Forge, to announce his exchange, and to congratulate him on the event, adding "we are again on the business of a general cartel with Mr. [sic] Howe."[1] The letter was franked by General

(1) The title evidently omitted by way of reciprocating similar incivilities of the British when they wrote to, or of, the American Commander-in-Chief.

Washington, and McHenry must have reported
at head quarters without delay, for on May 15th,
1778, he was appointed Secretary to the Commander-in-Chief.[1] He took as secretary, an oath
of allegiance to the United States and of renun-
ciation of George III, which is endorsed: "Sworn
before me this 9th June, 1778, Nath'l Greene, Maj.
Gen." His acquaintance with General Greene, and
the high esteem in which that officer held him,
may date from this time, though it is possible that
the efficient young Surgeon of Magaw's regiment,
may have come under his personal notice, when
Washington and Greene were frequently at or
about Fort Washington. From this time his relations with Washington were always most cordial,
and through life, Washington wrote to him as to
a trusted friend and adviser. McHenry's easy
and cheerful temper was able to bear the strain
which we may suppose must sometimes occur between two persons thrown so closely and constantly
together, in a position of social equality and of
military inequality, a strain which we know from
Hamilton's experience might become extreme when
Washington allowed his temper to escape from the
stern control under which it was generally kept.
The hero remained a hero to at least one of his

---

[1] He appears also to have returned at once to his duties as Surgeon, for
on May 17th, we find his old preceptor, Dr. Rush, writing to him as
"Senior Surgeon, Flying Hospital."

aides-de-camp, and it may be doubted whether Washington ever found a more devoted friend and follower than McHenry. Their correspondence shows that the intercourse between them, notwithstanding the difference in their years, must have been easier than Washington's reserved and inaccessible demeanor made possible with most men, for his letters to McHenry are marked by an affectionate, sometimes even by a playful tone, which we should hardly look for in the writer.

It would be altogether beyond the scope of this brief work to describe the campaigns in which McHenry was now to follow the fortunes of his chief, for this would be to write in large part, the history of the war during two eventful years, and it may be sufficient to say that he remained in Washington's military family until August, 1780, and that he was then transferred to La Fayette's staff, where he continued until the close of the war. This transfer showed the great confidence which Washington placed in McHenry, if the reason which we are about to give be the real one, namely, that Washington feared lest the youthful ardor of the Marquis, entrusted when not quite twenty-three years of age, with an important command, might outrun his discretion, and that he accordingly took the precaution of placing near him, one whom he knew to be a prudent adviser, and to whom more than three years' observation

of active campaigns may have given some insight
into the art of war. That McHenry himself be-
lieved, and later in life, notwithstanding his
habitual reserve, expressed his belief that such
were the reasons for placing him with La Fayette,
we learn from a record left by a young kinsman,
John McHenry,[1] whom we shall have further
occasion to quote. A letter from General Greene,[2]
July 24th, 1781, confirms this view. Greene was
at this time in command of the Southern department, comprising Virginia as well as the Carolinas,
and La Fayette was carrying on his Virginia campaign against Cornwallis, and although by reason
of the distance between the scene of their operations, La Fayette was practically independent of
Greene's control, he was yet nominally under his
direction, and corresponded with him as opportunity was given. Greene writes to "Dear Major"
[McHenry] from the High Hills of the Santee,
and advises with him as if he were a general in
command, rather than a staff officer, cautioning
him that "his lordship, [Cornwallis] is a modern
Hannibal, and is seeking for some capital advantage," &c. Further on:—"I wish you with me
exceedingly, but there is no inconvenience to which
I will not subject myself to oblige the Marquis. I

(1) John McHenry was educated for the law, and is known to Maryland lawyers by his work on Ejectments, and by Harris & McHenry's
Reports. He was Secretary of legation at the Hague in 1800.

(2) McHenry MSS.

3

am persuaded you are useful to him in moderating his military ardor." When it is remembered that Greene was an "intimate friend" of the commander,[1] this letter of advice to the aide-de-camp seems the more noteworthy. A previous letter of Greene's, to Washington, written from "Camp 1 May, 1781," shows still more clearly the estimation in which he held McHenry. He writes: "when I was appointed to the command of this army, I solicited Congress to give Dr. McHenry a majority that he might serve me in the character of Aid.[2] This they refused. I was persuaded when I made the application, of the necessity, and since have felt it most sensibly. Your Excellency can scarcely tell how happy you are in your family, and therefore can hardly judge of my situation. I cannot make a second application to Congress on the subject, nor should I have hopes of succeeding if I did; but I shall esteem it a peculiar mark of your Excellency's friendship and esteem, if you will interest yourself in the matter, and get him a majority. Your Excellency will judge of the propriety of my request," &c., &c. In 1785, McHenry furnished Dr. William Gordon, who was then engaged in writing a history of the

---

(1) Mémoires de La Fayette vol. i, p. 262.

(2) As he had already served as aid to the Commander-in-Chief, it was thought that he could not accept the same position with Gen. Greene without losing rank. "Nothing but a majority will engage him in this service."—G. W. Greene's Life of Nathaniel Greene, vol. iii, p. 44.

United States, with a memoir of the part taken
in the war by La Fayette, but it does not appear,
as indeed we should not expect under the circum-
stances, that he said anything in this memoir as
to the place which he himself was expected to fill
in the Marquis's military family. In his silence
on the subject it is not to be expected that much
evidence on this point could be forthcoming at
this day, but the above cited letter to him is
offered as worthy of consideration. Whether it
was due to La Fayette's own discretion or to the
"moderating" counsel of others, his caution was
as conspicuous as his courage. All accounts, says
Bancroft, "bear testimony to his prudence, and
that he never once committed himself during a
very difficult campaign." [1]

The promotion to the rank of Major which
Greene was so urgent about, must have followed
very close upon the receipt of his letter, if indeed it was not conferred independently of his or
Washington's application, for on May 30th, 1781,
his commission as Major was made out by Congress to date from the previous October.

McHenry was with La Fayette as aide-de-camp
when Arnold's treason was discovered, and on the
morning of September 24th, 1780, just before the
discovery took place, parting company with Washington and La Fayette, who went on to examine the

[1] History of the United States, vol. x, p. 507.

redoubts, he rode up to Arnold's head-quarters
to make Washington's apologies to Mrs. Arnold
about delaying breakfast. The party was still at
table when a hurried message was brought in to
Arnold, which caused him to mount his horse and
ride for his life.[1]

On March 7th, 1781, La Fayette, then on his way
to Virginia, on the expedition intended to crush
and capture Arnold, wrote to Washington from
Head of Elk: "The State of Maryland have made
to me every offer in their power. . . . . . Mr.
McHenry has been very active in accelerating the
measures of his State." The day before McHenry
had written a letter addressed to the merchants of
Baltimore, setting before them the urgent need of
material aid, whereupon a meeting was called and
a fund, to which he also contributed, was quickly
raised to defray expenses.

The intimacy begun between La Fayette and his
aide-de-camp was kept up through a friendly correspondence for a long time afterwards. In April,
1794, McHenry wrote to Washington, then President, a letter which may be read in Sparks's
Writings of Washington, vol. x, p. 398, suggesting

---

[1] It is perhaps worth mentioning that La Fayette's letter to the Cheva-
lier de la Luzerne, (Mémoires de La Fayette, vol. i, p. 367,) says : " nous
fûmes précédés par un de mes aides de camp et celui du Général Knox, qui
trouvèrent ce général et Madame Arnold à table," from which it would
appear that the account generally given, making Hamilton one of the two
aides-de-camp, must be incorrect. Hamilton's own letter, graphically
describing Mrs. Arnold's emotion *upon the discovery*, is quite reconcilable
with a later arrival.

the appointment of a commissioned person to be sent to Vienna to intercede for the release of La Fayette, at that time closely confined at Olmutz, with powers to proceed to France on a like errand in favor of his wife and children, but the appointment was not made.

Washington afterwards made direct intercession with the Emperor of Germany by letter, without success, and although in Parliament former foes of La Fayette generously protested against his imprisonment, and although chivalrous friends risked their lives and lost their liberty in attempting to rescue him, the imprisonment continued with accompaniments of great hardship, until Napoleon's arms, in 1797, forced a release. La Fayette revisited the United States as the "Nation's guest," in 1824, and when he came to Baltimore, where he was received with great enthusiasm and civic display, he landed first at Fort McHenry. In the brief reply which he made to the address of welcome, he alluded to the "confidential friend in my military family," of whom this fort "most nobly defended in the last war," brought back the "affecting recollection."[1]

On September 17th, 1781, when he must have been still with La Fayette, before Yorktown, McHenry was elected to the State Senate, and held his seat until he resigned early in 1786. In

[1] Scharf's Chronicles of Baltimore, p. 411.

May, 1783, he was appointed to Congress in place of Edward Giles, deceased, and was elected to the same position by the Legislature, on November 27th, 1783, was reëlected the following year, and held this office until 1786. This double duty, in State and Continental legislation, was not an uncommon thing in those days. In April, 1783, McHenry had some aspirations after diplomatic life, and there is a letter from Washington to him supporting his application to be official Secretary to the Court of London or Versailles, but McHenry not long afterwards became engaged to be married, and withdrew his application.

In 1787, he was one of the delegates from Maryland to the Convention which framed the Constitution, and of those chosen from his State, he was the first to take his seat. He was a regular and conscientious attendant, but does not seem to have taken much part in debate in this Convention, or probably, in the other deliberative bodies which he attended so many years, though we learn from letters which passed between him and Washington, while he was in Congress, in which he consulted his old Commander-in-Chief on important questions then pending, that he studied with attention the subjects of debate. ' He doubtless often conferred too with his old friend and correspondent, Hamilton, and it may safely be said that he gave his best efforts to have the Constitution accepted by the Convention, as he did afterwards to secure its adoption by the people of his own State. His efforts, and those of other prominent citizens, in behalf of the Constitution in Maryland, were, we need not say, successful, in spite of the earnest and able opposition of **Luther Martin** and **Samuel Chase**, and he was a member of the State Convention by which the Constitution was adopted in April, 1788. In the autumn of that year, McHenry was elected to the General Assembly of Maryland after a hotly contested canvass, and his success over his opponents, one of whom was Samuel Chase, was viewed as another triumph for the then rising Federal party.[1]

In 1789 he had the gratification of seeing his best hopes for the future of the federation realized, when on April 17th, General Washington passed through Baltimore on his way to New York, as

[1] The following extract from the Votes and Proceedings of the House of Delegates of Maryland for 1788, p. 17, is an amusing record of the action of the House in regard to a witness interested in an election bet:

THURSDAY, NOVEMBER, —— 1788.

"On motion, *Ordered, nem. con:* That the following be entered on the journal: That Mr. Charles Myers, previous to the assenting to the above resolution [a resolution as to said Myers's competency as a witness] was called as a witness on the part of the petitioners, and being sworn on the *voir dire*, whether he conceived himself interested in the decision of the House respecting the election for Baltimore town, answered that he betted two beaver hats previous to the last election, one that Mr. Chase would have a greater number of votes than Doctor McHenry, and the other that Mr. McMechen would have a greater number of votes than Doctor Coulter, and that he was not interested in any manner in the decision, unless only by such bets.

"Charles Myers having been examined on his *voir dire*, *Resolved:* That he is a competent witness."

President of the United States, and McHenry, who had been one of the committee of three, appointed by Congress at Annapolis to make suitable arrangements for the order of Washington's last public audience when he resigned his commission, was now on the committee which met and welcomed him in Baltimore at the outset of his new career. In the autumn of the same year McHenry was elected, without opposition, delegate to the General Assembly, and at the regular election of 1791, he was again sent to the Maryland Senate, and held his seat there till nearly the end of the term of five years, that is to say, until he became Secretary of War. This important office was conferred upon him by Washington in January, 1796, to fill the vacancy made by Timothy Pickering's promotion to the office of Secretary of State. Washington wrote to McHenry telling him frankly that he had already, "for particular reasons," offered the office to General Pinckney, to Colonel Carrington of Virginia, and to Governor Howard of Maryland. The first two were men in whose character and abilities Washington's letters show that he had a special confidence, the third—of whom Greene had written that "he deserved a statue of gold no less than the Roman and Grecian heroes"—was a friend and fellow-townsman of McHenry's, so there was no reason why the latter should be hurt at the manner of the offer, or at his place in this group of men whom Washington thought worthy of trust. He felt Washington's letter "as an injunction that he could not refuse," writes John McHenry, the young relative before mentioned, who was brought up in his household, "and most reluctantly accepted the appointment, leaving his pleasant retirement to embark in the troubled sea of politics." In the same letter Washington asks McHenry to sound Samuel Chase as to his accepting an appointment to the Supreme Court of the United States,—just as he had at the beginning of his administration written confidentially to his former Secretary to consult him on another judicial appointment,—and he thus had the satisfaction of being the intermediary through whom this important office was conferred upon his old opponent.

McHenry remained in office to the end of Washington's administration, and under President Adams, until a breach occurred between that President and his Secretary, which caused the latter to send in his resignation in May, 1800. His colleagues were Pickering, mentioned above, Oliver Wolcott, Secretary of the Treasury, and Charles Lee, Attorney General. In 1798, Benjamin Stoddert, of Maryland, was appointed Secretary of the newly constituted department of the Navy, but up to that time the administration of

4

naval affairs had devolved upon the Secretaries of War and of the Treasury, so that McHenry's office brought with it a full share of responsibility. The young country, relatively weak, was exposed to the jealousy of foreign powers, and while it had to be made ready generally against possible hostilities, in particular a war with France was for a long time imminent, and was actually begun on the seas by the capture of a French man of war. The relations with that country were highly critical, and the great difficulty of the situation was that the Anti-federalists sympathised so fully with the republic across the water, that her most flagrant outrages on American commerce, her grossest defiance of the government, her most indecent violations of international duties, were easily pardoned, were almost applauded. "Whatever France did, it approved; whatever France desired, it was ready to grant," wrote McHenry many years afterwards of the opposition party of that day, a party moreover which considered the military power a dangerous engine in the hands of the central government, and resisted on principle the establishment of any effective army or navy. The Federalists were at this time the war party, and McHenry shared their unwillingness to put up with repeated wrongs and insults at the hands of the sister republic. He did all in his power to put the country in a state of readiness, by building and equipping powerful frigates, which were destined to prove their prowess in a later war, by erecting armories and arsenals and by establishing the Military Academy at West Point. He also caused to be delivered up, according to treaty stipulations, the Spanish posts on the western waters, which had still been held under various pretexts.

When Washington was appointed Commander-in-Chief of the army for the threatened war with France, McHenry was despatched by Adams to Mount Vernon, in July, 1798, to inform him of it, and to confer with him as to the appointment of his officers. He had with McHenry a full understanding on the subject, and, stipulating that if he was to be Commander-in-Chief he should have the power of naming the general officers under him, he indicated as his choice, Hamilton for the second in command, and Pinckney and Knox to be Major Generals next in rank. The President used many efforts to change this arrangement, giving as his reason the respect which was due to Knox on account of his seniority in the former service, but really moved, as Hamilton's friends thought, by an anxious jealousy of the influence and popularity of the rival leader of the Federal party, and by a fear that his brilliant talents for war would win a still more overshadowing distinction for one already eminent both as statesman and financier. Wash-

ington adhered to his position, and was supported
by the whole cabinet, who finally brought Adams
to reason. From this time the President felt a
certain amount of distrust of his cabinet officers,
as he knew them to be strong friends of Hamilton,
and supporters generally of his measures, but in
spite of this feeling on Adams's part, his personal
relations with his Secretaries were maintained on a
pleasant footing. He wrote, it is true, to the Secretary of War, while the question of the precedence
among the generals was still under advisement,
"there has been too much intrigue in this business
both with General Washington and me. If I shall
ultimately be the dupe of it, I am much mistaken
in myself"; but when his Secretary promptly
wrote back, asking whether these intrigues, if any
had been employed, were imputed to him, offering
to convince the President that he had not been
concerned in any, or, on failure so to convince him,
offering to retire at once from a situation which
demanded a perfect and mutual confidence between
the President and the person filling it, Adams
withdrew the imputation, having "no scruple to
acknowledge that his conduct throughout the whole
towards him had been candid." Such a withdrawal
of the charge of intrigue on this occasion, it would
seem ought to be considered final, but the distinguished biographer of Mr. Adams has thought fit
to revive the charge, and has attempted to show

that "the remark itself was entirely just."[1] For-
tunately he refers us at the places cited, to the
authorities, the correspondence on which he relies,
and with much confidence we refer to the same for
his refutation, convinced that the candid reader
will decide that they utterly fail to support the
charge. If it were disaffection to have a strong
conviction that Hamilton was the fittest man to
be placed next in command to Washington, then
McHenry and the other Secretaries were disaf-
fected, if it were intrigue to express this conviction, they were intriguers. Let us waive the
argument furnished by the weight of Washington's name, which would supply the answer that
if there was a plot he was the chief conspirator,
and let us put Mr. Adams to the proof of the
following propositions, none of which do we think
his arguments or his authorities will enable him
to establish: first, that the Secretaries did not
really believe that the interests of the country
called for Hamilton as the fittest man for the
place; secondly, that so believing it was not their
duty to say so, and thirdly, that as a matter of
fact they were not justified in their belief.

It would call for a greater space than this occasion will allow, to sketch even in outline the leading questions of that day, or the differences between

(1) Life and works of John Adams. By Charles Francis Adams. Vol.
viii, pp. 588–594.

the President and his cabinet regarding them. To go into any discussion of the alien and sedition laws, of the rupture of relations with France, of the humiliating and grotesque story of the X, Y, Z intrigues, of the preparations for war, of the President's sudden change of policy in resuming negotiations, would be to enter upon a chapter in our history which has been expounded often enough already by partizan writers, and although some of the vexed questions may now be settled, this is not the time for recording how they have been settled. That the personal relations of the President and his cabinet were still sufficiently friendly, is shown by a letter from McHenry to Washington, written in November, 1799. "The President believes, and with reason, that three of the heads of departments have viewed the mission [to France] as impolitic and unwise. I find that he is particularly displeased with Mr. Pickering and Mr. Wolcott, seemingly a little less so with me, yet those he is so displeased with, are still received and treated by him with apparent cordiality."

This apparent cordiality was not to last many months longer. The rupture was to be brought about upon a personal, not upon a political, issue. A cabinet which differences on important public questions had failed to disunite, was to be broken up by reason of the President's jealousy of disposition. Jealousy was a prominent, nay a pre-dominant trait in Adams's nature. It needs no careful analysis of his character, no ill-natured inferences from his conduct to prove this. His own speeches, his own letters prove it beyond con-tradiction. It may be said of him, roughly speak-ing, that he was jealous of every great man he came in contact with, that the contemplation of their greatness embittered him during their lives and haunted him when they were in their graves. He had been jealous of Franklin, he had been jealous of Washington, and he was jealous with what has been called a "frantic jealousy" of Ham-ilton. Three of the Secretaries, Pickering, Wol-cott and McHenry, during Adams's administration, as previously under Washington's, had been in the habit of consulting with Hamilton, who was regarded by the President, it is true, as a personal rival, but was nevertheless, by the general consent of his contemporaries, not only the head and front of the Federal party but also one of the foremost men of his time. The President had long smarted under this fancied grievance, and when he found his popularity waning, and his hold on the party's allegiance slipping away, his smouldering jealousy at last burst forth. The Secretary of War was made the first victim of his wrath. He was sent for by the President, a stormy interview took place in which his resignation was requested, and it was accordingly sent in the next day.[1] Pickering followed in a few days, Wolcott after an interval. McHenry's place was filled by Samuel Dexter, of Massachusetts.

Now as to the conduct of the Secretaries in consulting with Hamilton on the general questions of the day, its propriety needs no defence. In times fraught with great danger to the country, it was their duty not only as party men but as patriots, to ask the ablest exponent of Federal principles for advice which he was always ready to give, never dismayed by the vastness of a subject nor repelled by its minuteness of detail, and if such a man happened to be personally unacceptable to the President it was a thing they could very properly disregard.

But another question has become involved with this one. Just before the President's breach with his Secretaries, the Federal leaders had determined that it should be the policy of their party that each of their electors should vote at the approaching election for both Mr. Adams and General Pinckney for President, without giving one the preference over the other. Under the existing provisions of the Constitution we do not see what other plan could have been adopted, but the difficulty in the problem was that in case of a solid vote for either of the candidates, a single defection from the other would lose him the election. Adams's unpopularity in some quarters made it very possible that he might be the victim, though in fact he received one vote more than Pinckney, while both were beaten by Jefferson and Burr. Of course here was room for intrigue, and in the President's mind, room for suspicion of intrigue, in which Hamilton must be chief conspirator and the Secretaries his willing tools. Adams made no charge of such intrigue in his interview with the Secretary of War, though in his anger he made accusations much more frivolous. We do not know that he ever made such charges afterwards. Surely with his keen scent for a grievance, if there was one there he would have found it out. He even expressed himself about McHenry in a manner intended to disclaim such a charge. But again his distinguished biographer is not satisfied. "Recent disclosures," says Mr. C. F. Adams,[1] "prove that McHenry had not merited this generosity. He certainly was one, though the least important, of the three cabinet ministers who were untrue to him and who betrayed his confidence. . . . He furnished Mr. Hamilton with a part of the confidential matter used by him in his pamphlet, and he entered warmly into the cabal to defeat Mr. Adams's reëlection." Mr. C. F. Adams then refers "for the

[1] Life and Works of John Adams, vol. ix, p. 53, note.

evidence to sustain all these views" to certain letters to be found in Gibbs's work, but the reader referring to the authorities given for these "recent disclosures," will again be surprised to find that they utterly fail to support Mr. Adams's statement. They disclose, it is true, that McHenry wrote Hamilton an account of Adams's absurd explosion of temper, but is it seriously pretended that angry words which would be insolence from any one else, are a confidential communication from a President? But the letters do not disclose, and Mr. C. F. Adams has not shown, nor is it the fact, that McHenry had any consultations with Hamilton, or any one else, looking towards Adams's defeat at the next election, *until after he had left the Cabinet.* "For my own part," writes McHenry, at the time of his retirement, "I had never taken a single step to depreciate his character, or prevent his election, or expressed any public disapprobation of the mission [to France.]" But suppose the fact to be otherwise, let it be remembered that here is no charge, as we understand it, about divulging State secrets or lines of policy, it is simply a personal matter; it is not a question as to faithful adherence to the interests and policy of an existing chief magistrate, it is a question of the selection of a future chief magistrate. Is it possible that a Secretary's position in the Cabinet forbids him to discuss confidentially with an intimate friend of

twenty years standing, the character of a President and his fitness to be a candidate for reëlection, matters of vital consequence to his party,
and, as he thinks, to his country? And if he
writes, is he to use only the language of diplo-
macy, or of eulogy, or is he to write as he feels?
And when he leaves office, and for an indefinite
time thereafter, are he and his correspondents to
be characterized as a cabal, is his criticism an
intrigue, and his blame a betrayal? Let the
answer to these questions, if they deserve an answer, be given in the words of Charles Carroll,
writing about Adams to McHenry, in November,
1800: "I conceive it a species of treason to con-
ceal from the public his incapacity."[1] And apart
from his duty to the public, if for his own vindication a retired Cabinet officer is ever justified in
setting forth his record and placing the responsibility where it should properly rest, such a course
may be allowed to the Cabinet officers of an
Executive who so constantly ignored them or dis-
regarded their advice.

A few more words must still be devoted to Mr.
C. F. Adams's work, on account of the extraor-
dinary interpretation therein put upon one of
McHenry's letters. The note last above cited,[2]
concludes thus: "It is, however, no more than

(1) Works of Alexander Hamilton, by J. C. Hamilton, vol. vi, p. 479.
(2) Vol. ix, p. 53.

due to him [McHenry,] to add that of all the
parties to it, ['the cabal' just mentioned,] his
letters betray the most profound sense of the
degrading measures they resorted to. He desig-
nates their conduct as 'tremulous, timid, feeble,
'deceptive and cowardly. They write private let-
'ters. To whom? To each other...... They
'meditate in private. Can good come out of such
'a system? If the party recovers its pristine
'energy and splendor, shall I ascribe it to such
'cunning, paltry, indecisive, back-door conduct?'"
We do not like to accuse Mr. Adams of garbling
extracts, but the mutilated citation here has the
same effect. He has just spoken of the three
Cabinet Ministers who "betrayed" the President's
"confidence," and has mentioned McHenry's correspondence with Hamilton, then he charges that
McHenry entered into "the cabal to defeat Mr.
Adams's reëlection,"—a small cabal, (for the biographer has had the advantage of examining the letters of *all* of them,) and presumably consisting of
Hamilton and the three Secretaries, for they are
the only individuals named—, then, to show that
McHenry was the most conscience-stricken of this
*cabal*, he quotes him as designating *their* conduct
as "tremulous," &c. "They write," &c. But we
turn to the letter itself, given in Gibbs's work,
vol. ii, p. 384, only to find that the writer is dis-
cussing not a cabal, but the *whole Federal party*.

"Have our party shown that they possess the necessary skill. . . . . . Their conduct . . . . is tremulous. . . . . They write. . . . They meditate," &c. We call upon Mr. Adams to correct his quotation before issuing the next edition of his work, and at the same time we invite him to consider whether it will, when corrected, in any way help to prove his point. Mr. Adams's argument must be: McHenry condemns the conduct of the Federal party, McHenry is a member of that party, *ergo*, McHenry condemns himself. It is a tolerably familiar form of rhetorical appeal for a speaker or writer to identify himself with the objects of his criticism and to represent both himself and them as sharing in the blame which attaches to a certain course. Mr. Adams belongs to a family of writers and orators, and has doubtless himself used that form of appeal, but we venture to give a trite example. Cassius speaks of himself and the other Romans as peeping about, "to find ourselves dishonorable graves." But even the perverted ingenuity of a Shakesperian commentator never found in this line an admission at all damaging to Cassius's personal honor, nor can the unbiassed reader find the faintest admission of a sense of degradation implied in McHenry's strictures on the Federal party.

But this is already a well worn controversy.
Pickering and Wolcott have long since been more
than sufficiently vindicated, and there is no occasion to be strong upon the stronger side, by
going further into the defence of a third member
of the Cabinet, whom Adams himself regarded
as the least hostile of the three. It may be said
of them, we think the judgment of history has
already said of them, that they were actuated by
patriotic, and not by selfish motives, and that they
deserved well of a country which, in a trying and
formative period, they served with purity, devotion
and courage. Indeed, it may be supposed that the
long and close friendship with Washington, which
each of these men enjoyed, was of itself a sufficient
guarantee of their personal honor and political integrity. Certainly, they seem to have retained the
approval of a good conscience and of each other,
they remained firm friends and frequent correspondents, and cherished for some time their hopes
of saving the country by means of the Federal
party, even, if need be, without Mr. Adams.
"Your retiring from the office you have so long
filled, will not lose you one of your real friends,"
writes McHenry to Wolcott, in December, 1800.
"As for the rest, take leave of them all kindly.
.... I insist upon your eating dinner with me
in Baltimore, on your way home, and wish you
so to arrange the time and company that two

or three of our Connecticut friends in Congress
may accompany you. You must not deny me
this favor. Your true and affectionate friend,"
&c. McHenry's relations with Hamilton were
always most cordial, and the two friends continued to correspond and consult in crises of
political affairs, as when Hamilton wrote to him
during the "Tie intrigues," to use his influence
with the Maryland Federalists, that the electoral
vote of that State should be cast for Jefferson,
the known foe, rather than for Burr, the already
suspected traitor.

McHenry's letter of resignation to the President
concluded thus:

"Having discharged the duties of Secretary of
War for upwards of four years with fidelity, unre-
mitting assiduity, and to the best of my abilities, I
leave behind me all the records of the department,
exhibiting the principles and manner of my official
conduct, together with not a few difficulties I have
had to encounter. To these written documents I
cheerfully refer my reputation as an officer and a
man."

It is probable that he thus fairly enough
summed up the character of his administration
of the War office, and that his management of it
was marked more by fidelity and industry than
by any conspicuous talent for conducting the
complicated affairs of a great department. The

organizing faculty is a rare one, and does not
necessarily go along with a sound judgment of
men and principles, or with readiness in action
in individual cases. He had accepted the office
unwillingly, he had exercised it faithfully under
"not a few difficulties,"—among them President
Adams's growing discouragement of any thorough
preparation of the country for war,—and he
gladly left it to return to more congenial pur-
suits, "my old employments, reading and rural
occupations." Within a few months we find him
writing to his friend Wolcott to discuss with him
not party politics but the improvement of the
apple culture, and to quote to him from Philips's
Cider rather than from the Federal Gazette.

The dissensions in the cabinet were but a small
part of McHenry's difficulties as a public man.
He had to meet the bitter opposition of the
Anti-federalists while he was in office, and their
unsparing criticism afterwards when their party
became a majority in Congress. A committee
was appointed in December, 1801, to enquire into
the management of the War Department and its
expenditure of funds. The committee of investigation made an unfavorable report, April 29th,
1802, and four days after, Congress adjourned.
McHenry feeling himself aggrieved by their report, prepared an elaborate defence in "A Letter
to the Honourable the Speaker of the House of

Representatives," with accompanying documents, which was read in the next session of that body, December 28th, 1802, by the Speaker, Nathaniel Macon, and was also printed for private circulation among the author's friends. A copy of this Letter may be seen in the Maryland Historical Society's Library. We think that any candid reader will decide from such study of the facts as may be made at this day, that the committee's investigation was not for the purpose of discovering and reporting the truth, but was a partisan effort to "make political capital," and that McHenry's defence is as successful as it is spirited. The pamphlet begins with explaining how the unjust charges which the committee's report had set in motion, had at length compelled him "to relinquish a silence become too painful, a silence perhaps incompatible with a due regard to my own character, a due consideration for my family and friends, and with the profound gratitude and veneration with which I am penetrated for the memory of that departed Patriot who first called me, after an intimate acquaintance commenced in my youth, to the administration of the Department of the War." Then follows an examination *seriatim* of the charges contained in the committee's report. The first of the charges, involving at the most a mere error of judgment, was that too much money had been spent on a military laboratory or arsenal built near Philadelphia for the purpose of making and storing arms and munitions of war. This charge seems to have been fairly met and answered. Another, much more serious, that the Secretary's accounts were not properly settled, and that large balances were due from him, was completely disposed of, and a long array of figures and accounts was produced in his vindication. The paltriness of the next charge is in keeping with the spirit of the whole report. It appears that certain sums of money, $1320 in all—it was a day of small things—had been spent in some secret service, and although the President, Adams, had vouched for the propriety of the expenditures, the committee fastened upon this record that any disbursement had been made for undisclosed services, as showing that a wrong principle and presumably corrupt practices prevailed in the administration of the war office. There is a refreshing sarcasm in McHenry's treatment (p. 46 of the Letter) of the implied argument that the United States ought never to use this baleful "secret service" to meet the machinations of French diplomatists and the cunning of Indian braves:

"What, may I be permitted to ask, is there in the nature of our people, or of our government, that calls for publicity in transactions which no other government would publish? Is ours a gov-

ernment which can repose in apathy and set at
defiance foreign intrigue and hostility, and which,
from its colossal strength, stands in need of no
secret operations to discover the one or obviate
the other? Is ours a government in which a
secret may be told to the whole people, and yet
remain a secret to the people and government of
other countries? Are transactions, in their nature
and essence private and confidential, involving
many and various persons and interests, to be
exposed to the examination of a series of clerks,
to be recorded in a public office, and the agents
to be betrayed?

"I beseech gentlemen to reconsider the hope
with which they have vainly flattered themselves.
To view men and things as they are. To come
forth, and instead of directing the thunder of
their censure against the late administration,
acknowledge in the spirit of candor and good
sense, and after considering the various occasions
that must have originated within these few years
past demanding such disbursements, how little,
how very little in this way has been expended."

After disposing effectually of still another charge
of the investigating committee, so petty that it is
not worth while to record its refutation, the pamphlet ends with this vigorous passage:

"It was my lot to be entrusted with the direction
of the Department of War for a course of time,

during a great part of which the affairs of this country were considerably agitated. Whether the Department was administered well or ill, whether such of the plans projected by me as were carried into execution, and, others offered by me to the consideration of the councils of the United States, have, or would probably have, in their results conduced to the public benefit, must be committed to time and the dispassionate judgment of others to decide. I have not vanity sufficient to flatter myself that while in office I was always right, and never surprised into error; too well do I know that it is impossible to conduct a great and complicated department so as always to avoid mistakes. My own mind does however derive satisfaction from a review of my endeavors for the public good, and I confidently trust I have shewn that any errors justly ascribable to me, are not those imputed in the report of the committee of investigation."

"I close this letter, resting in the hope that the members of the honorable the House of Representatives, mindful of the alternate victories of parties, which have harassed, disgraced, and destroyed so many governments, will nobly signalize the period of their preëminence,[1] by the dignity of their candor and inflexible justice."

[1] Alluding to the existing anti-federalist majority.

McHenry appears to have taken little or no part in public life after this time. He was a man who did not court notoriety or power, but being of refined tastes and quiet habits, preferred elegant ease in private life to the turmoil of a political career. He had married January 8th, 1784, Margaret, daughter of David Caldwell, of Philadelphia, and had a family growing up about him. He lived at his country place, Fayetteville, named by him after his former Commander, a mile west of the Court House, in Baltimore. Part of his estate has resisted as yet, the builder's invading march of improvement, and remains a pleasant *rus in urbe*, in the possession of Mr. Thomas Winans. "Although he was fond of leisure," writes John McHenry, "there was nothing slothful in his temperament. "While in office, he was indefatigable in his official duties, and after his retirement from office he spent most of his time in reading and keeping pace with the train of political events in this country and Europe." In the year 1807, he published a Directory of Baltimore City. He wrote in 1811, a political pamphlet, "The Three Patriots," the characters portrayed being Jefferson, Madison and Monroe. The motive of the work may be found in the remark (p. 30,) that in the French vocabulary, those citizens or subjects only of a foreign nation devoted to France, are called patriots, all the others partizans of England, monarch[ist]s, or aristocrats," followed by a quotation from a letter of Minister Fauchet's, speaking of Jefferson, Madison and Monroe as "worthy of that imposing title." In the only place in which the author speaks of Adams in this pamphlet, he calls him "that eminent character, long known and revered for talents and integrity.[1]

About this time he was a good deal occupied in writing a book after the plan of the Travels of Anacharsis, a work which he admired. He kept the manuscript to himself, but the impression was that the work had, in spite of its classical dress, an American application. We are left to conjecture however as to its character and merits, for the manuscript being put, with other important papers, into a trunk to be taken to his son's place in the country, where the author hoped to find quiet and time for writing, the trunk and its contents were lost and never heard of again, and after this discouragement, he did not resume the work. In 1813, we hear of Dr. McHenry as the President of the first Bible Society formed in Baltimore.

He took no part in the war of 1812, to which, like many leading Federalists, he was opposed.

(1) This pamphlet, and also the Directory, are in the Maryland Historical Society's Library.

It happens, however, that through the defence of Fort McHenry, commemorated in the Star Spangled Banner, his name is closely linked with the best remembered incident of the war. His son, John McHenry, was engaged in the defence of Baltimore, serving as ensign at the battle of North Point.

During the war he wrote, evidently after a long interval, to his old friend Pickering, at this time a member of Congress. His letter[1] is dated July 24th, 1813, from Cherry Tree Meadows, a place in "the Glades" of Alleghany County, Maryland, where he had established his eldest son, Daniel Wm. McHenry. "My dear Sir: When we labored together in the same cabinet for the public welfare, I conceived for you a real esteem and sincere friendship. . . . . The calumnies that have since assailed you (in which I have also partook) as I knew them to be unmerited and unfounded, could in no way lessen this esteem." . . . He then speaks of his "Letter," which was read in the House of Representatives, and adds: "I had a number of copies of this letter printed, but I distributed only a few of them, with an injunction not to publish their contents. This is the only notice I ever took of these calumnies, public or private. Religion, I thank God, enabled me to forgive their inventors. . . . . This is perhaps the last letter I shall

(1) Life of Timothy Pickering, by Charles W. Upham, vol. iv, p. 229.

ever write you. I have, it is true, gained a little strength, which will encourage me to try whether by short stages, I can regain my old home. My children there are extremely desirous to see me, I also wish to see them. . . . . May God lengthen your days, without mingling with them pains, sorrows or misfortunes. . . Your affectionate friend, James McHenry."

But his health seems to have been more fully restored than he then hoped. Two years and a half later, Pickering writes to his wife: "Washington, December 19th, 1815. I have concluded to pass Christmas at Baltimore, according to my first intention. My excellent friend Mr. McHenry, by the enclosed letter has reminded me of my promise to dine with him on Christmas Day, and kindly invites me to lodge with him. I shall do both."

On the 3d of May, in the following year, Dr. James McHenry died at his suburban home, in the 63d year of his age. He left surviving him his wife and two children, his son John and daughter Anna, married to James Pillar Boyd, his eldest son, Daniel, having died before him.

www.ingramcontent.com/pod-product-compliance
Lightning Source LLC
Chambersburg PA
CBHW021238260626
47172CB00002B/824